DATE DUE

PRINTED IN U.S.A.

[redacted]

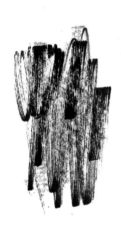

SKYLANDERS

RETURN OF THE DRAGON KING

PART 2: THE MENACE OF MALEFOR

Written by:
RON MARZ and **DAVID A. RODRIGUEZ**

Art by:
FICO OSSIO

Colors by:
DAVID GARCIA CRUZ

Letters by:
DERON BENNETT

ABDOPUBLISHING.COM

Reinforced library bound edition published in 2019 by Spotlight, a division of ABDO
PO Box 398166, Minneapolis, Minnesota 55439. Spotlight produces high-quality
reinforced library bound editions for schools and libraries.
Published by agreement with IDW.

Printed in the United States of America, North Mankato, Minnesota.
042018
092018

THIS BOOK CONTAINS
RECYCLED MATERIALS

ACTIVISION. IDW

Originally published as SKYLANDERS issue #8.

Library of Congress Control Number: 2017961398

Publisher's Cataloging in Publication Data

Names: Marz, Ron, author. Rodriguez, David A., author. | Ossio, Fico; Cruz, David Garcia; Baldeón, David, illustrators.
Title: Return of the dragon king / writers: Ron Marz and David A. Rodriguez; art: Fico Ossio; David Garcia Cruz; David Baldeón.
Description: Reinforced library bound edition. | Minneapolis, MN : Spotlight, 2019 | Series: Skylanders set 2 | Part 1: All's fairy in love and war written by Ron Marz and David A. Rodriguez; illustrated by Fico Ossio and David Garcia Cruz. | Part 2: The menace of Malefor written by Ron Marz and David A. Rodriguez; illustrated by Fico Ossio and David Garcia Cruz. | Part 3: Reach for the sky written by Ron Marz and David A. Rodriguez; illustrated by Fico Ossio, David Baldeón & David Garcia Cruz.
Summary: Join your favorite Skylanders heroes in these all-new comic book adventures! Spyro, Cynder, and Hex discover their powers were stolen by a mysterious fairy to revive a malevolent and powerful enemy.
Identifiers: ISBN 9781532142468 (Part 1: All's fairy in love and war) | ISBN 9781532142475 (Part 2: The menace of Malefor) | ISBN 9781532142482 (Part 3: Reach for the sky)
Subjects: LCSH: Skylanders (Game)--Juvenile fiction. | Monsters--Juvenile fiction. | Rescues--Juvenile fiction. | Dragon--Juvenile fiction. | Race--Juvenile fiction. | Escapes--Juvenile fiction. | Imaginary wars and battles--Juvenile fiction. | Comic books, strips, etc.--Juvenile fiction.
Classification: DDC 741.5--dc23

ABDO
Spotlight

A Division of ABDO
abdopublishing.com

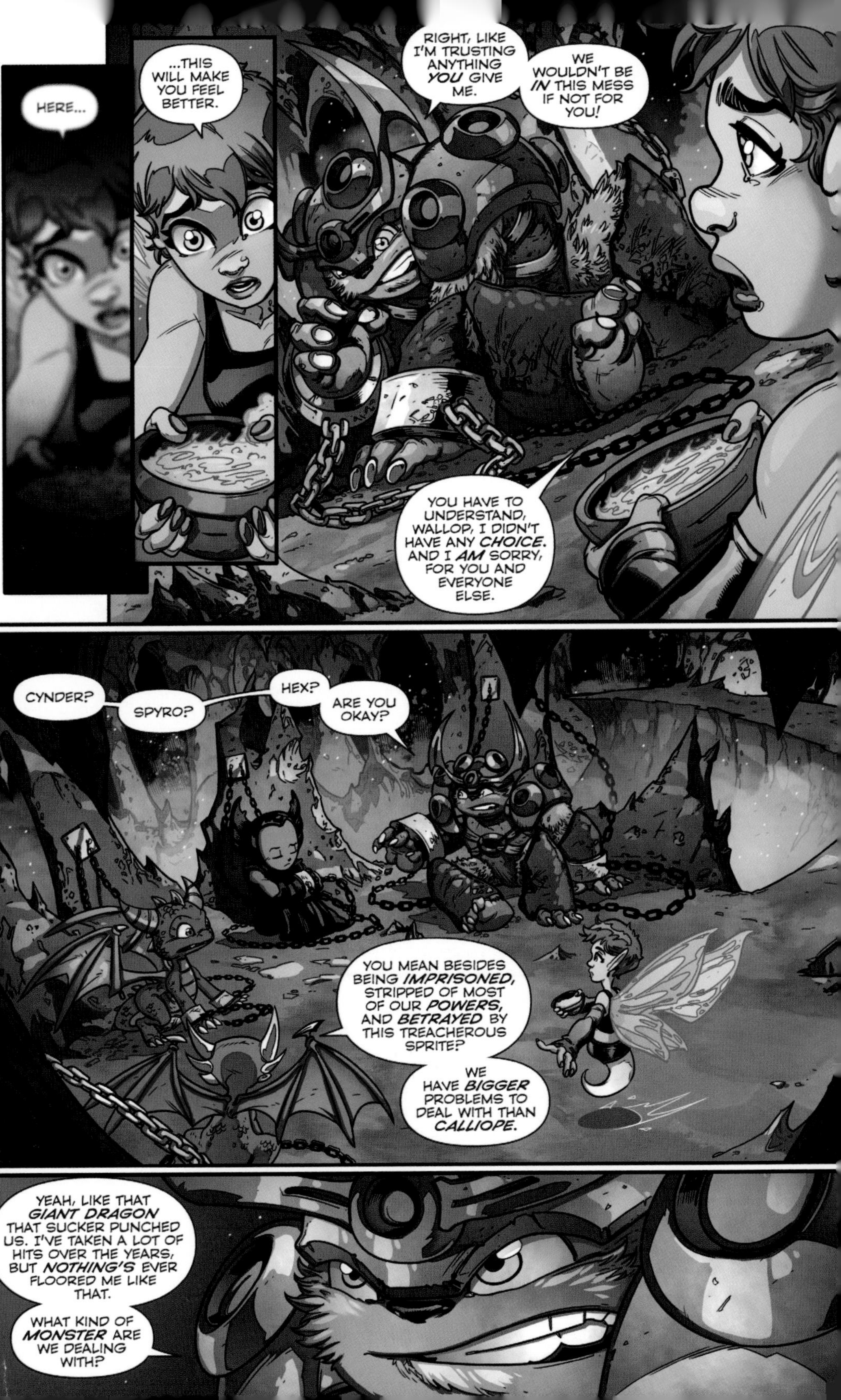
HERE...
...THIS WILL MAKE YOU FEEL BETTER.
RIGHT, LIKE I'M TRUSTING ANYTHING YOU GIVE ME.
WE WOULDN'T BE IN THIS MESS IF NOT FOR YOU!
YOU HAVE TO UNDERSTAND, WALLOP, I DIDN'T HAVE ANY CHOICE. AND I AM SORRY, FOR YOU AND EVERYONE ELSE.
CYNDER?
SPYRO?
HEX?
ARE YOU OKAY?
YOU MEAN BESIDES BEING IMPRISONED, STRIPPED OF MOST OF OUR POWERS, AND BETRAYED BY THIS TREACHEROUS SPRITE?
WE HAVE BIGGER PROBLEMS TO DEAL WITH THAN CALLIOPE.
YEAH, LIKE THAT GIANT DRAGON THAT SUCKER PUNCHED US. I'VE TAKEN A LOT OF HITS OVER THE YEARS, BUT NOTHING'S EVER FLOORED ME LIKE THAT.
WHAT KIND OF MONSTER ARE WE DEALING WITH?

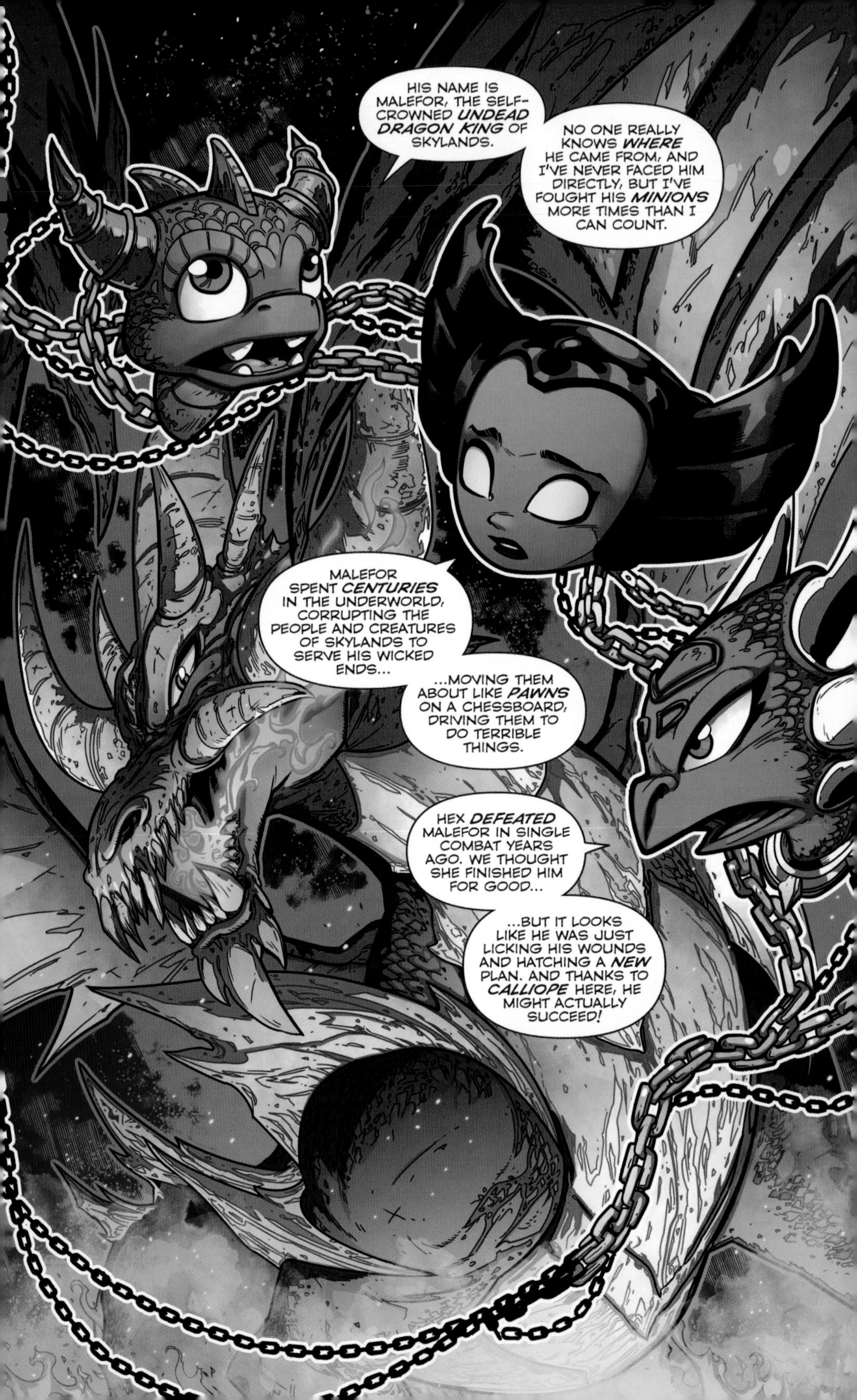
HIS NAME IS MALEFOR, THE SELF-CROWNED *UNDEAD DRAGON KING* OF SKYLANDS.
NO ONE REALLY KNOWS *WHERE* HE CAME FROM, AND I'VE NEVER FACED HIM DIRECTLY, BUT I'VE FOUGHT HIS *MINIONS* MORE TIMES THAN I CAN COUNT.
MALEFOR SPENT *CENTURIES* IN THE UNDERWORLD, CORRUPTING THE PEOPLE AND CREATURES OF SKYLANDS TO SERVE HIS WICKED ENDS...
...MOVING THEM ABOUT LIKE *PAWNS* ON A CHESSBOARD, DRIVING THEM TO DO TERRIBLE THINGS.
HEX *DEFEATED* MALEFOR IN SINGLE COMBAT YEARS AGO. WE THOUGHT SHE FINISHED HIM FOR GOOD...
...BUT IT LOOKS LIKE HE WAS JUST LICKING HIS WOUNDS AND HATCHING A *NEW* PLAN. AND THANKS TO *CALLIOPE* HERE, HE MIGHT ACTUALLY SUCCEED!

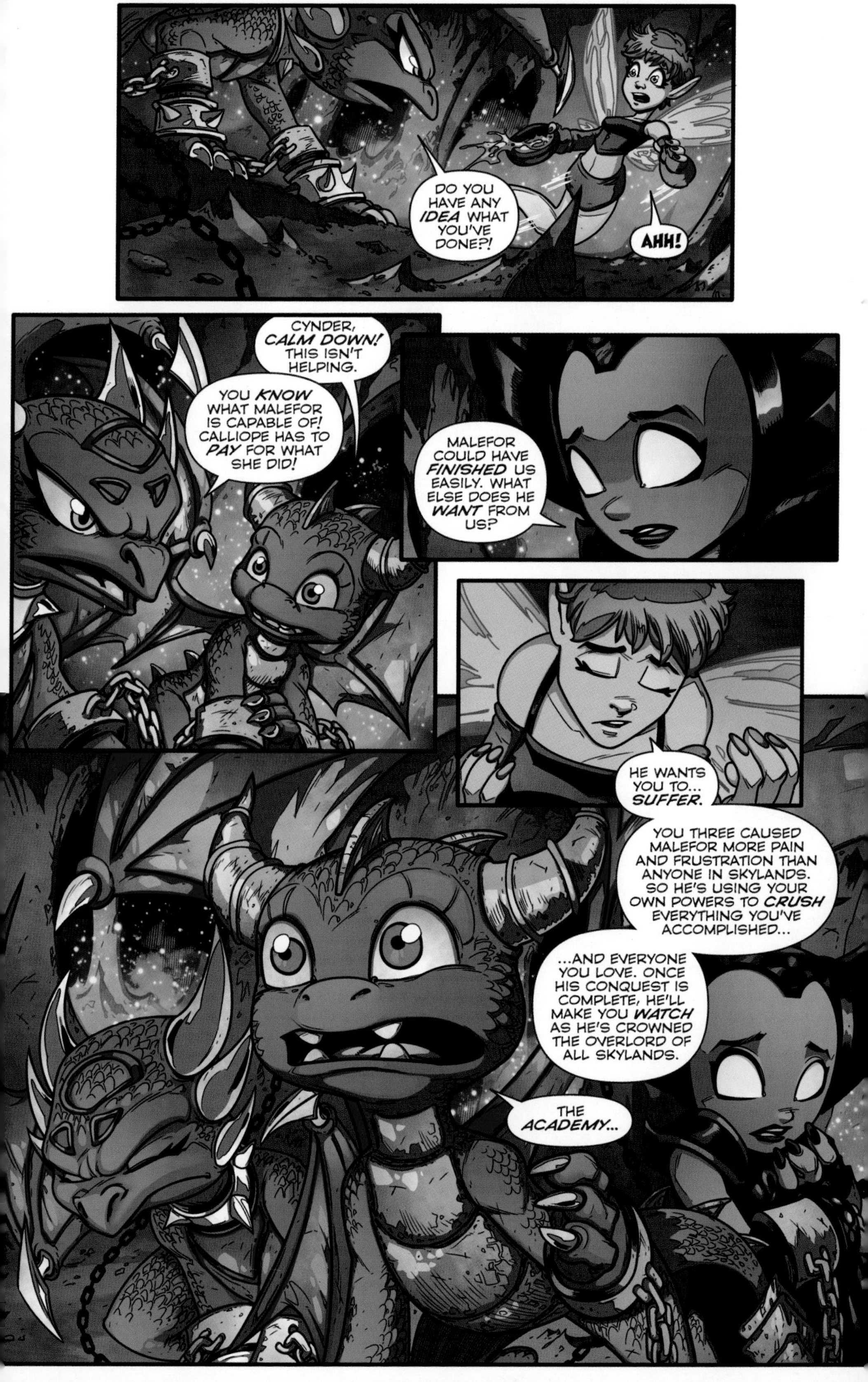
DO YOU HAVE ANY *IDEA* WHAT YOU'VE DONE?!
AHH!
CYNDER, *CALM DOWN!* THIS ISN'T HELPING.
YOU *KNOW* WHAT MALEFOR IS CAPABLE OF! CALLIOPE HAS TO *PAY* FOR WHAT SHE DID!
MALEFOR COULD HAVE *FINISHED* US EASILY. WHAT ELSE DOES HE *WANT* FROM US?
HE WANTS YOU TO... *SUFFER*.
YOU THREE CAUSED MALEFOR MORE PAIN AND FRUSTRATION THAN ANYONE IN SKYLANDS. SO HE'S USING YOUR OWN POWERS TO *CRUSH* EVERYTHING YOU'VE ACCOMPLISHED...
...AND EVERYONE YOU LOVE. ONCE HIS CONQUEST IS COMPLETE, HE'LL MAKE YOU *WATCH* AS HE'S CROWNED THE OVERLORD OF ALL SKYLANDS.
THE *ACADEMY*...

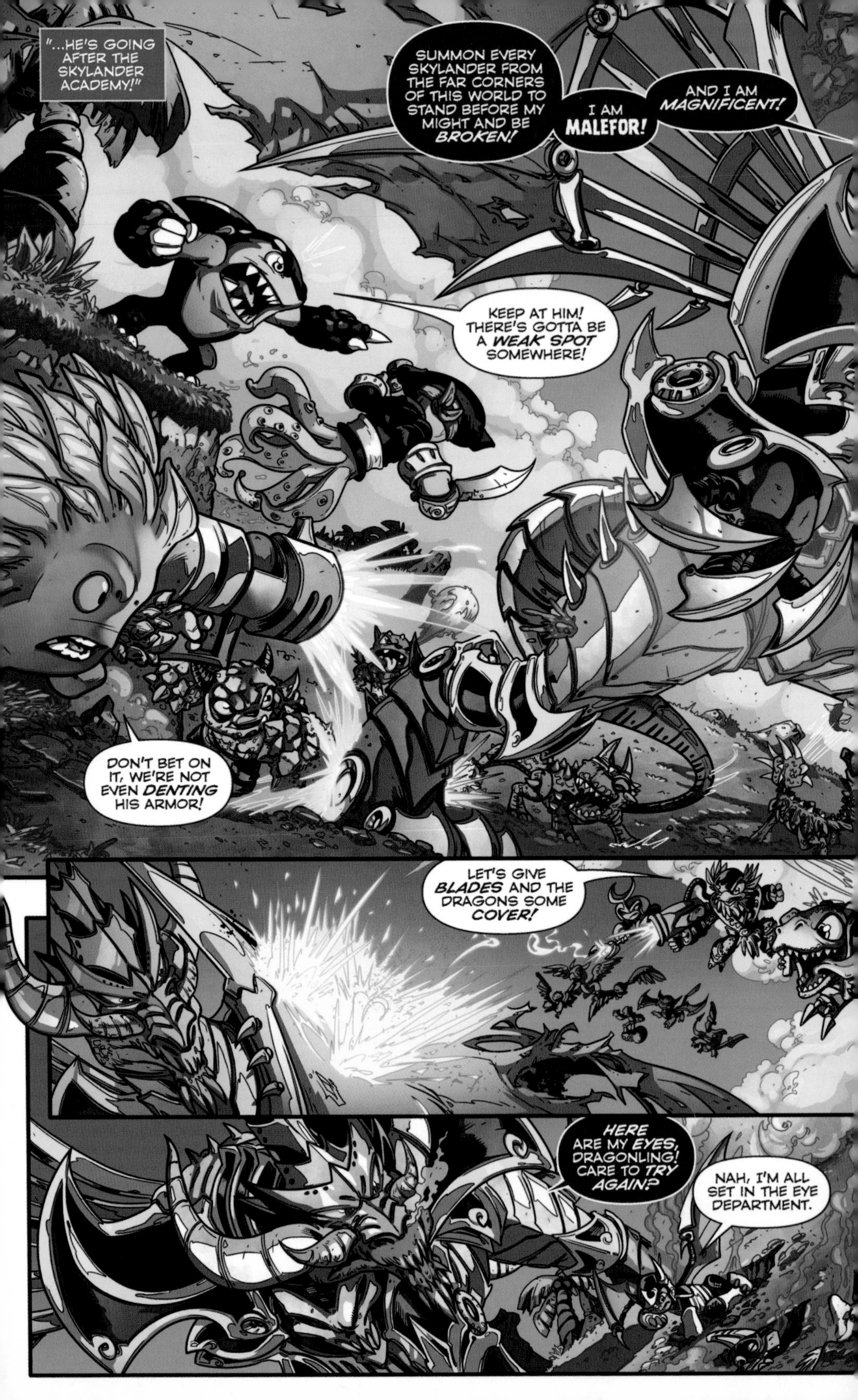
"...HE'S GOING AFTER THE SKYLANDER ACADEMY!"
SUMMON EVERY SKYLANDER FROM THE FAR CORNERS OF THIS WORLD TO STAND BEFORE MY MIGHT AND BE BROKEN!
I AM MALEFOR!
AND I AM MAGNIFICENT!
KEEP AT HIM! THERE'S GOTTA BE A WEAK SPOT SOMEWHERE!
DON'T BET ON IT, WE'RE NOT EVEN DENTING HIS ARMOR!
LET'S GIVE BLADES AND THE DRAGONS SOME COVER!
HERE ARE MY EYES, DRAGONLING! CARE TO TRY AGAIN?
NAH, I'M ALL SET IN THE EYE DEPARTMENT.

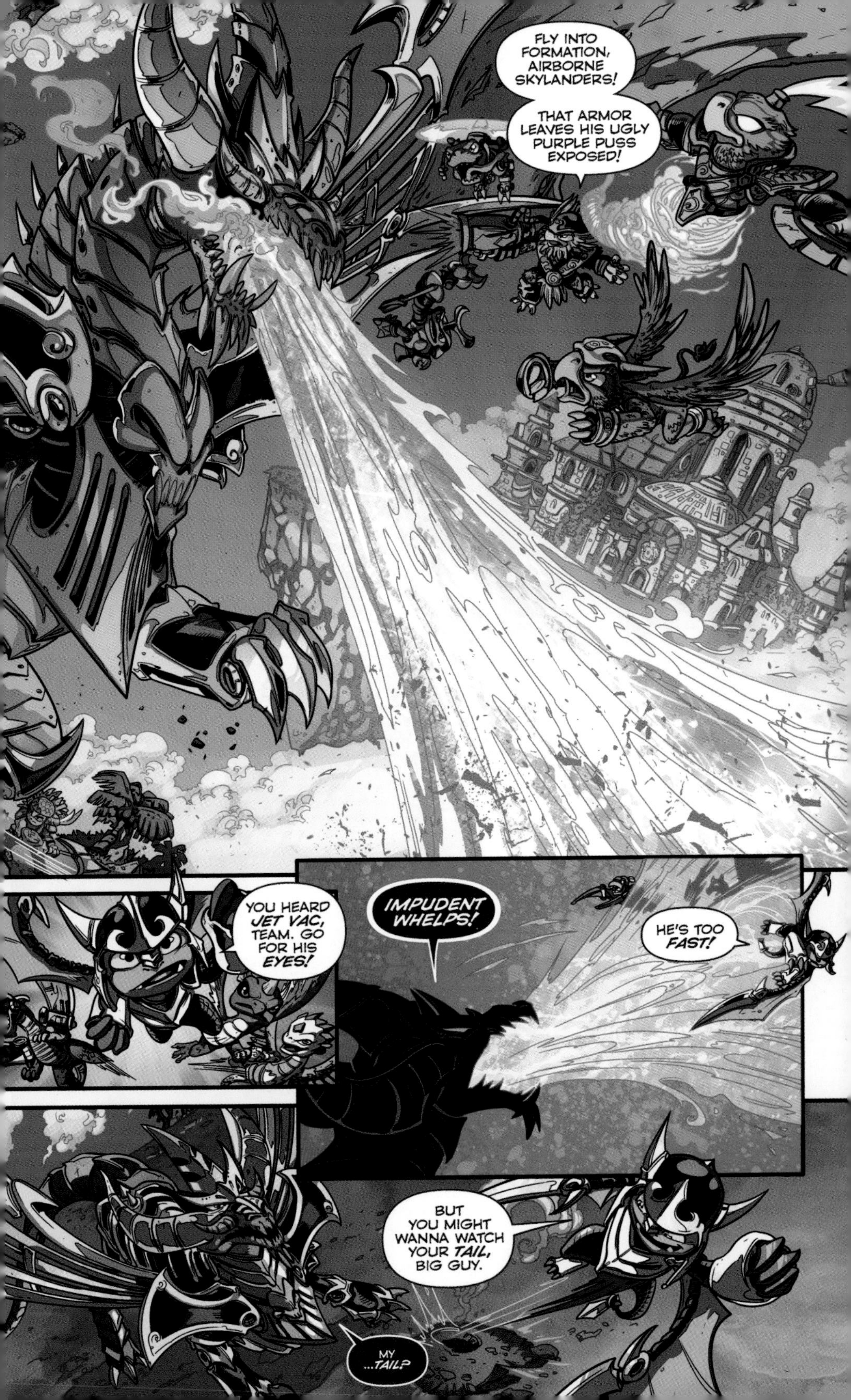
FLY INTO FORMATION, AIRBORNE SKYLANDERS!
THAT ARMOR LEAVES HIS UGLY PURPLE PUSS EXPOSED!
YOU HEARD *JET VAC*, TEAM. GO FOR HIS *EYES!*
IMPUDENT WHELPS!
HE'S TOO *FAST!*
BUT YOU MIGHT WANNA WATCH YOUR *TAIL*, BIG GUY.
MY ...*TAIL?*

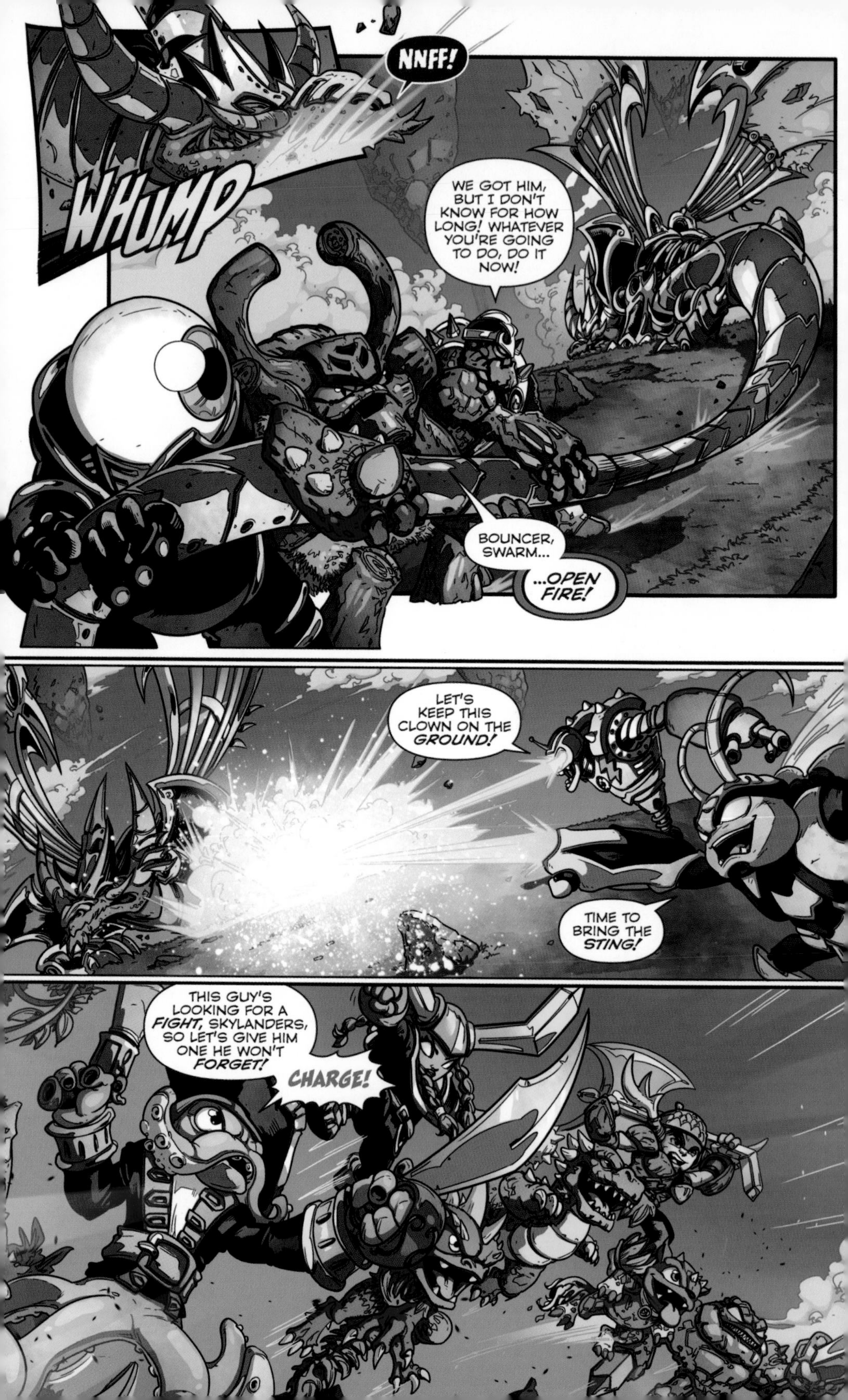
NNFF!
WHUMP
WE GOT HIM, BUT I DON'T KNOW FOR HOW LONG! WHATEVER YOU'RE GOING TO DO, DO IT NOW!
BOUNCER, SWARM...
...OPEN FIRE!
LET'S KEEP THIS CLOWN ON THE GROUND!
TIME TO BRING THE STING!
THIS GUY'S LOOKING FOR A FIGHT, SKYLANDERS, SO LET'S GIVE HIM ONE HE WON'T FORGET!
CHARGE!

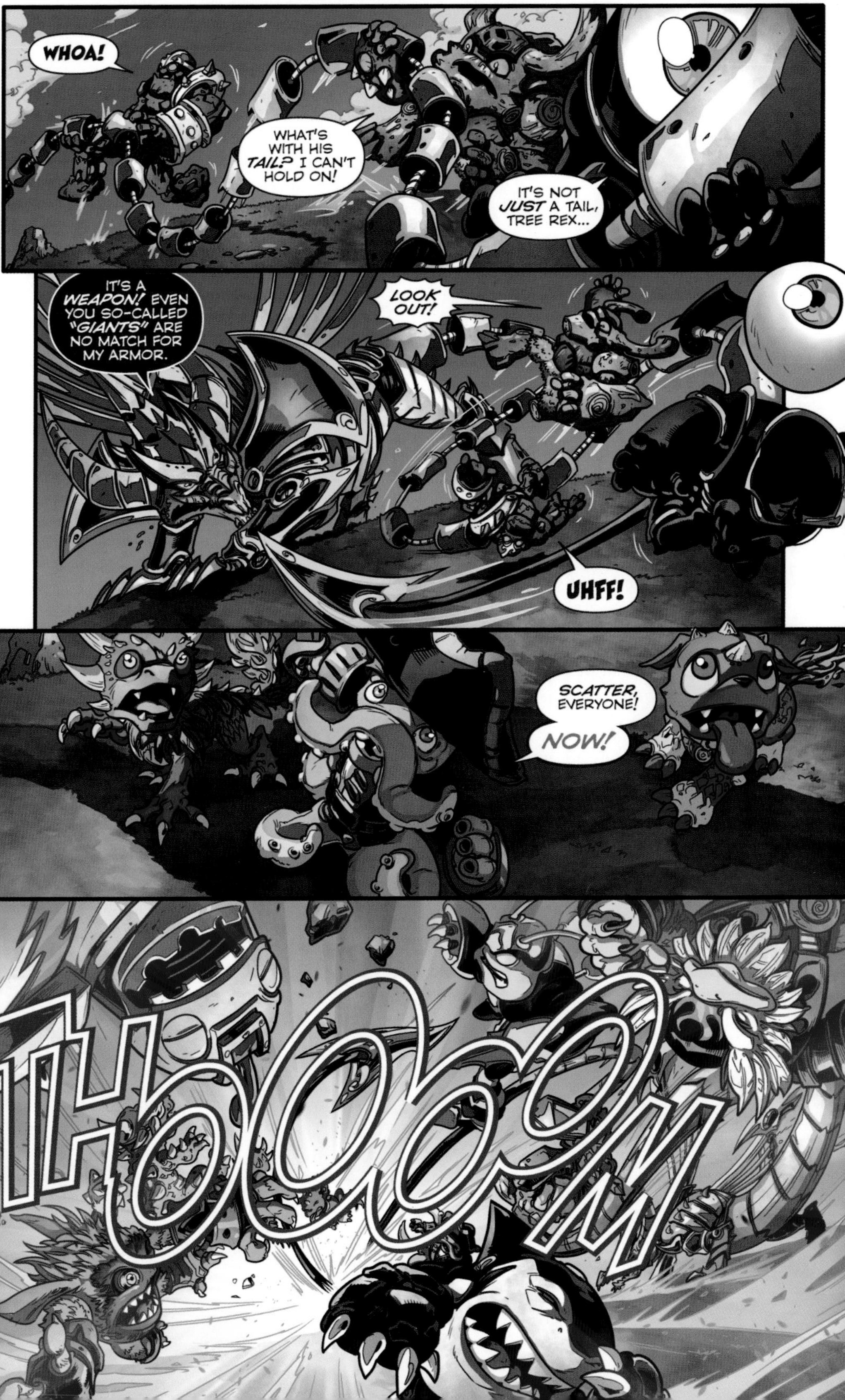
WHOA!
WHAT'S WITH HIS TAIL? I CAN'T HOLD ON!
IT'S NOT JUST A TAIL, TREE REX...
IT'S A WEAPON! EVEN YOU SO-CALLED "GIANTS" ARE NO MATCH FOR MY ARMOR.
LOOK OUT!
UHFF!
SCATTER, EVERYONE!
NOW!
THOOOM

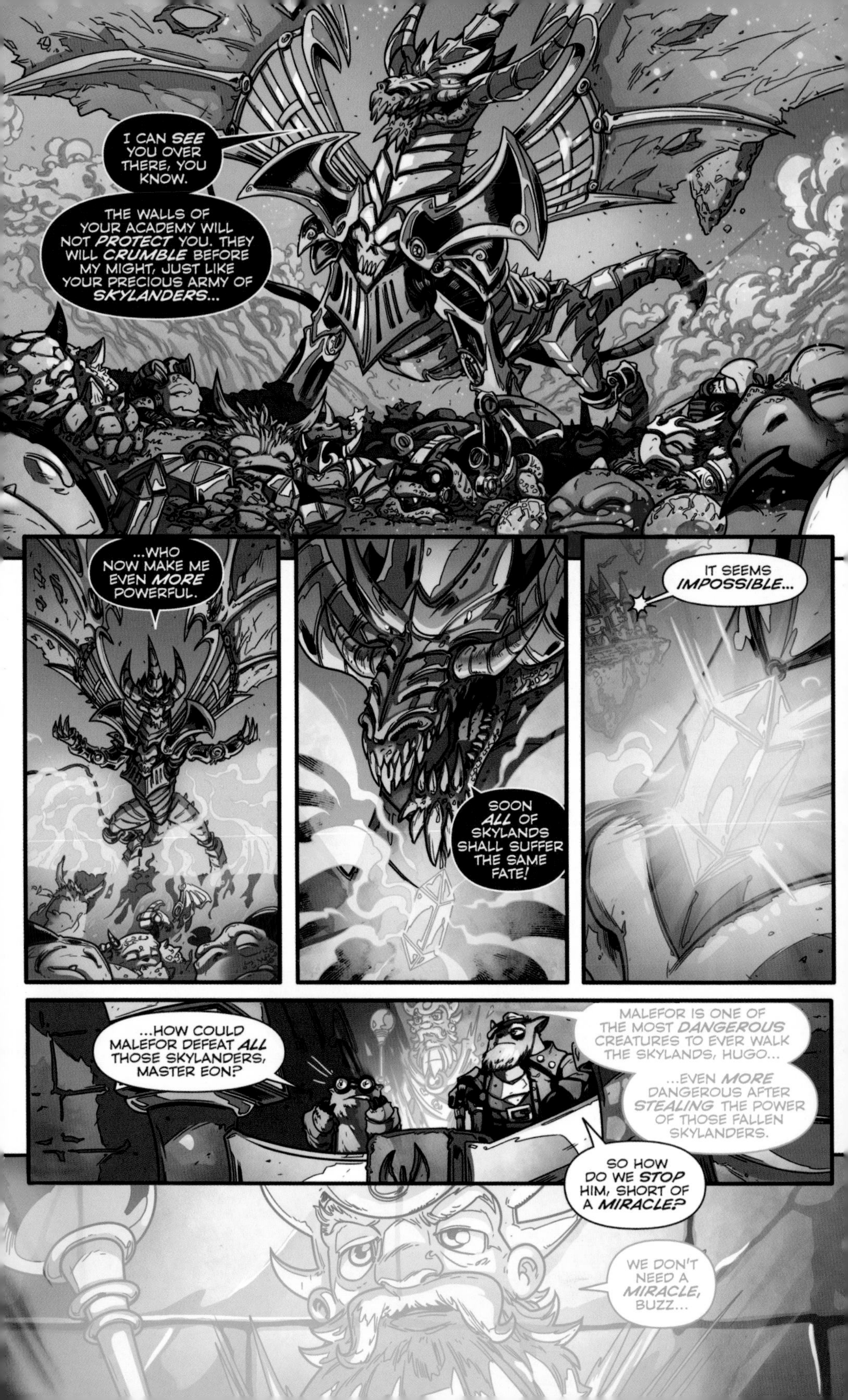

I CAN SEE YOU OVER THERE, YOU KNOW.
THE WALLS OF YOUR ACADEMY WILL NOT PROTECT YOU. THEY WILL CRUMBLE BEFORE MY MIGHT, JUST LIKE YOUR PRECIOUS ARMY OF SKYLANDERS...
...WHO NOW MAKE ME EVEN MORE POWERFUL.
SOON ALL OF SKYLANDS SHALL SUFFER THE SAME FATE!
IT SEEMS IMPOSSIBLE...
...HOW COULD MALEFOR DEFEAT ALL THOSE SKYLANDERS, MASTER EON?
MALEFOR IS ONE OF THE MOST DANGEROUS CREATURES TO EVER WALK THE SKYLANDS, HUGO...
...EVEN MORE DANGEROUS AFTER STEALING THE POWER OF THOSE FALLEN SKYLANDERS.
SO HOW DO WE STOP HIM, SHORT OF A MIRACLE?
WE DON'T NEED A MIRACLE, BUZZ...

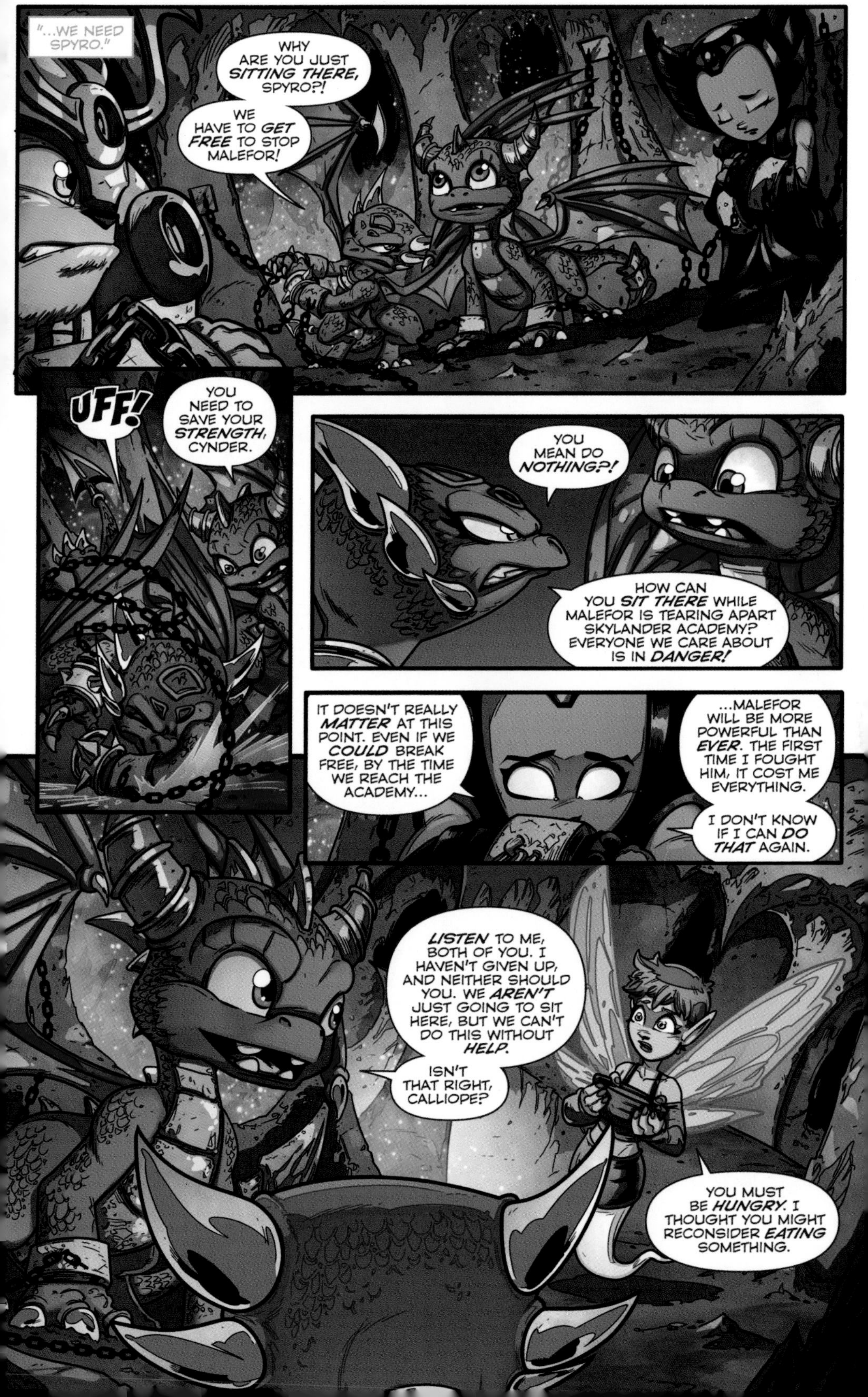
"...WE NEED SPYRO."
WHY ARE YOU JUST SITTING THERE, SPYRO?!
WE HAVE TO GET FREE TO STOP MALEFOR!
UFF!
YOU NEED TO SAVE YOUR STRENGTH, CYNDER.
YOU MEAN DO NOTHING?!
HOW CAN YOU SIT THERE WHILE MALEFOR IS TEARING APART SKYLANDER ACADEMY? EVERYONE WE CARE ABOUT IS IN DANGER!
IT DOESN'T REALLY MATTER AT THIS POINT. EVEN IF WE COULD BREAK FREE, BY THE TIME WE REACH THE ACADEMY...
...MALEFOR WILL BE MORE POWERFUL THAN EVER. THE FIRST TIME I FOUGHT HIM, IT COST ME EVERYTHING.
I DON'T KNOW IF I CAN DO THAT AGAIN.
LISTEN TO ME, BOTH OF YOU. I HAVEN'T GIVEN UP, AND NEITHER SHOULD YOU. WE AREN'T JUST GOING TO SIT HERE, BUT WE CAN'T DO THIS WITHOUT HELP.
ISN'T THAT RIGHT, CALLIOPE?
YOU MUST BE HUNGRY. I THOUGHT YOU MIGHT RECONSIDER EATING SOMETHING.

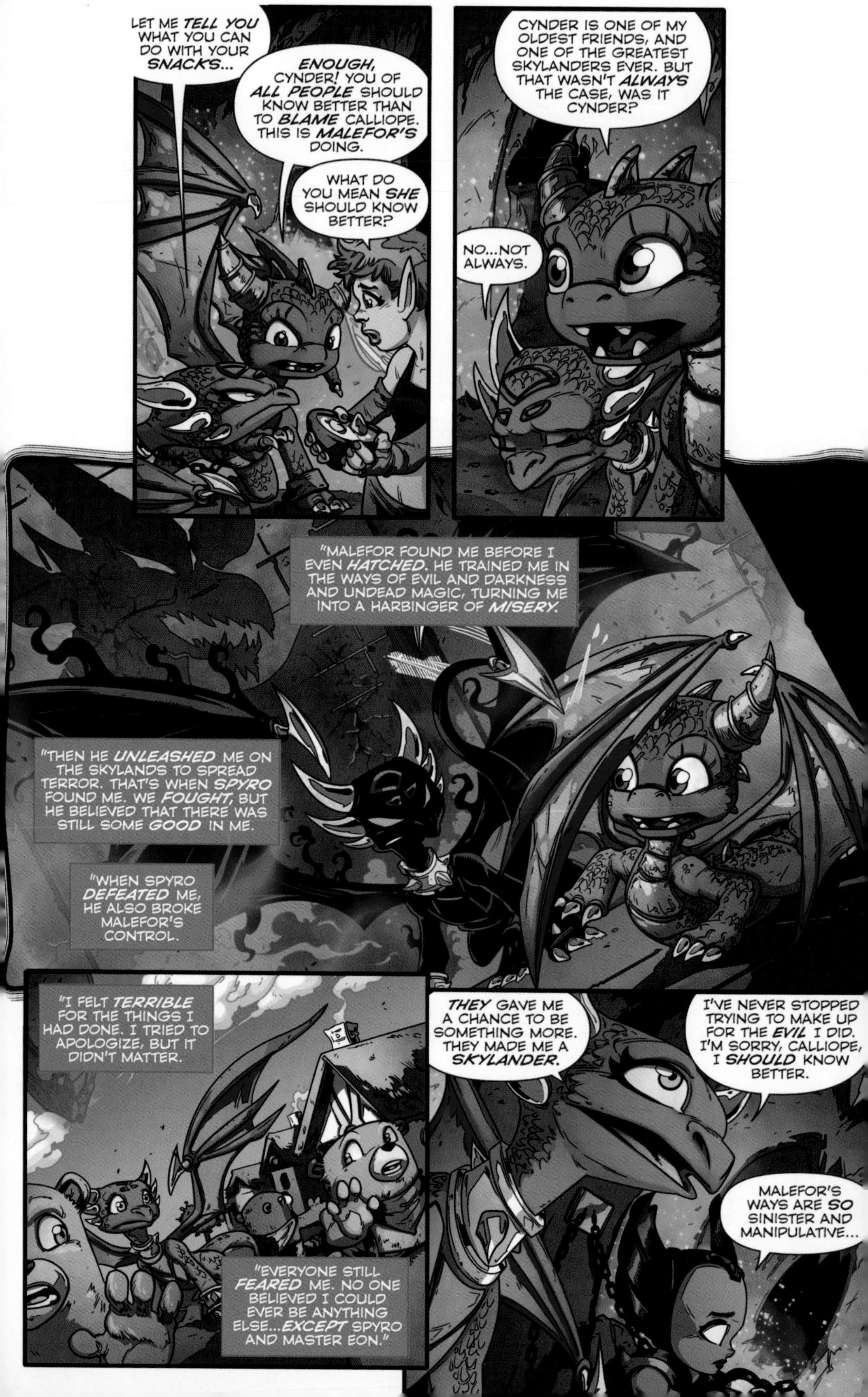
LET ME TELL YOU WHAT YOU CAN DO WITH YOUR SNACKS...
ENOUGH, CYNDER! YOU OF ALL PEOPLE SHOULD KNOW BETTER THAN TO BLAME CALLIOPE. THIS IS MALEFOR'S DOING.
WHAT DO YOU MEAN SHE SHOULD KNOW BETTER?
CYNDER IS ONE OF MY OLDEST FRIENDS, AND ONE OF THE GREATEST SKYLANDERS EVER. BUT THAT WASN'T ALWAYS THE CASE, WAS IT CYNDER?
NO...NOT ALWAYS.
"MALEFOR FOUND ME BEFORE I EVEN HATCHED. HE TRAINED ME IN THE WAYS OF EVIL AND DARKNESS AND UNDEAD MAGIC, TURNING ME INTO A HARBINGER OF MISERY.
"THEN HE UNLEASHED ME ON THE SKYLANDS TO SPREAD TERROR. THAT'S WHEN SPYRO FOUND ME. WE FOUGHT, BUT HE BELIEVED THAT THERE WAS STILL SOME GOOD IN ME.
"WHEN SPYRO DEFEATED ME, HE ALSO BROKE MALEFOR'S CONTROL.
"I FELT TERRIBLE FOR THE THINGS I HAD DONE. I TRIED TO APOLOGIZE, BUT IT DIDN'T MATTER.
"EVERYONE STILL FEARED ME. NO ONE BELIEVED I COULD EVER BE ANYTHING ELSE...EXCEPT SPYRO AND MASTER EON."
THEY GAVE ME A CHANCE TO BE SOMETHING MORE. THEY MADE ME A SKYLANDER.
I'VE NEVER STOPPED TRYING TO MAKE UP FOR THE EVIL I DID. I'M SORRY, CALLIOPE, I SHOULD KNOW BETTER.
MALEFOR'S WAYS ARE SO SINISTER AND MANIPULATIVE...

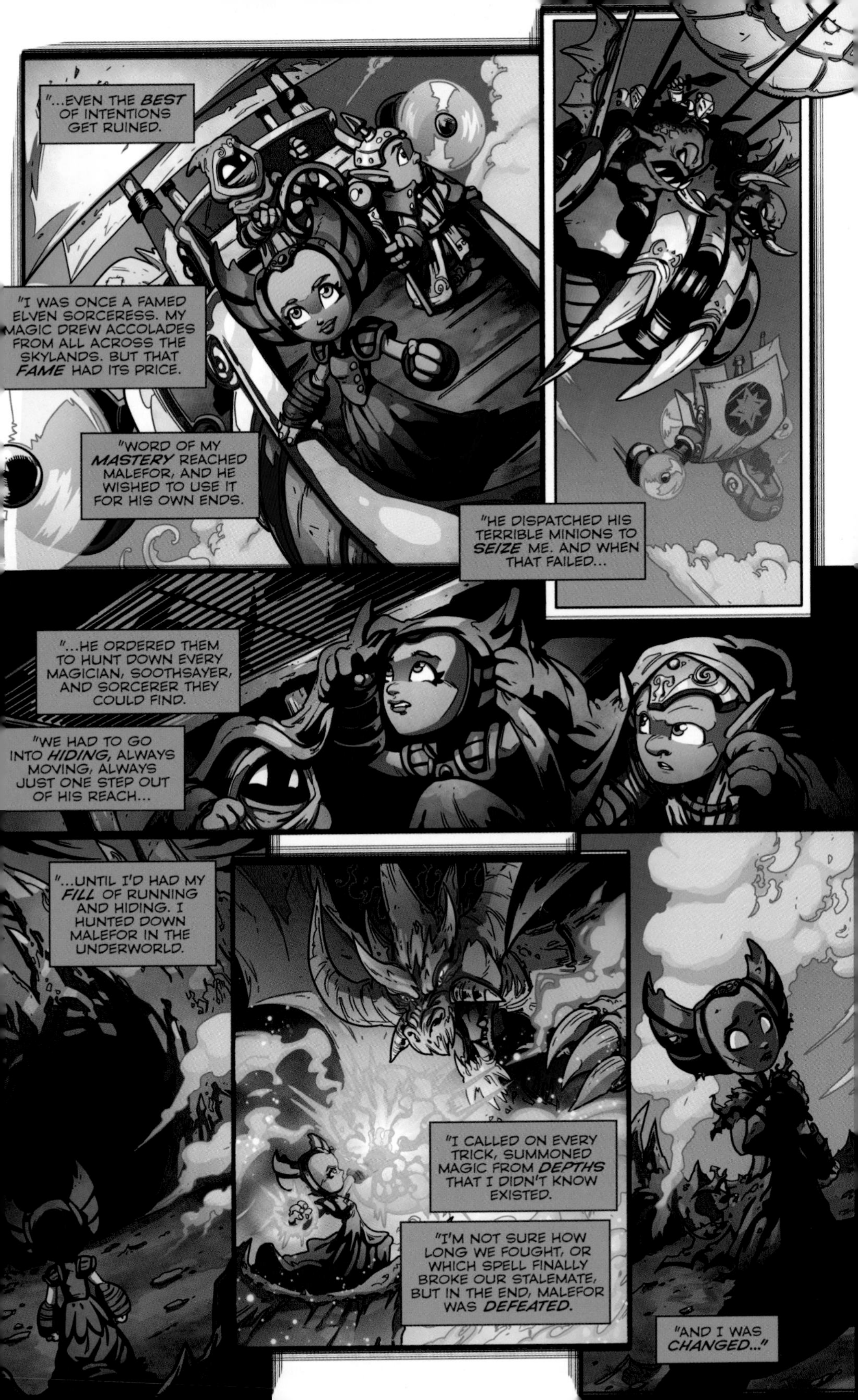
"...EVEN THE BEST OF INTENTIONS GET RUINED.
"I WAS ONCE A FAMED ELVEN SORCERESS. MY MAGIC DREW ACCOLADES FROM ALL ACROSS THE SKYLANDS. BUT THAT FAME HAD ITS PRICE.
"WORD OF MY MASTERY REACHED MALEFOR, AND HE WISHED TO USE IT FOR HIS OWN ENDS.
"HE DISPATCHED HIS TERRIBLE MINIONS TO SEIZE ME. AND WHEN THAT FAILED...
"...HE ORDERED THEM TO HUNT DOWN EVERY MAGICIAN, SOOTHSAYER, AND SORCERER THEY COULD FIND.
"WE HAD TO GO INTO HIDING, ALWAYS MOVING, ALWAYS JUST ONE STEP OUT OF HIS REACH...
"...UNTIL I'D HAD MY FILL OF RUNNING AND HIDING. I HUNTED DOWN MALEFOR IN THE UNDERWORLD.
"I CALLED ON EVERY TRICK, SUMMONED MAGIC FROM DEPTHS THAT I DIDN'T KNOW EXISTED.
"I'M NOT SURE HOW LONG WE FOUGHT, OR WHICH SPELL FINALLY BROKE OUR STALEMATE, BUT IN THE END, MALEFOR WAS DEFEATED.
"AND I WAS CHANGED..."

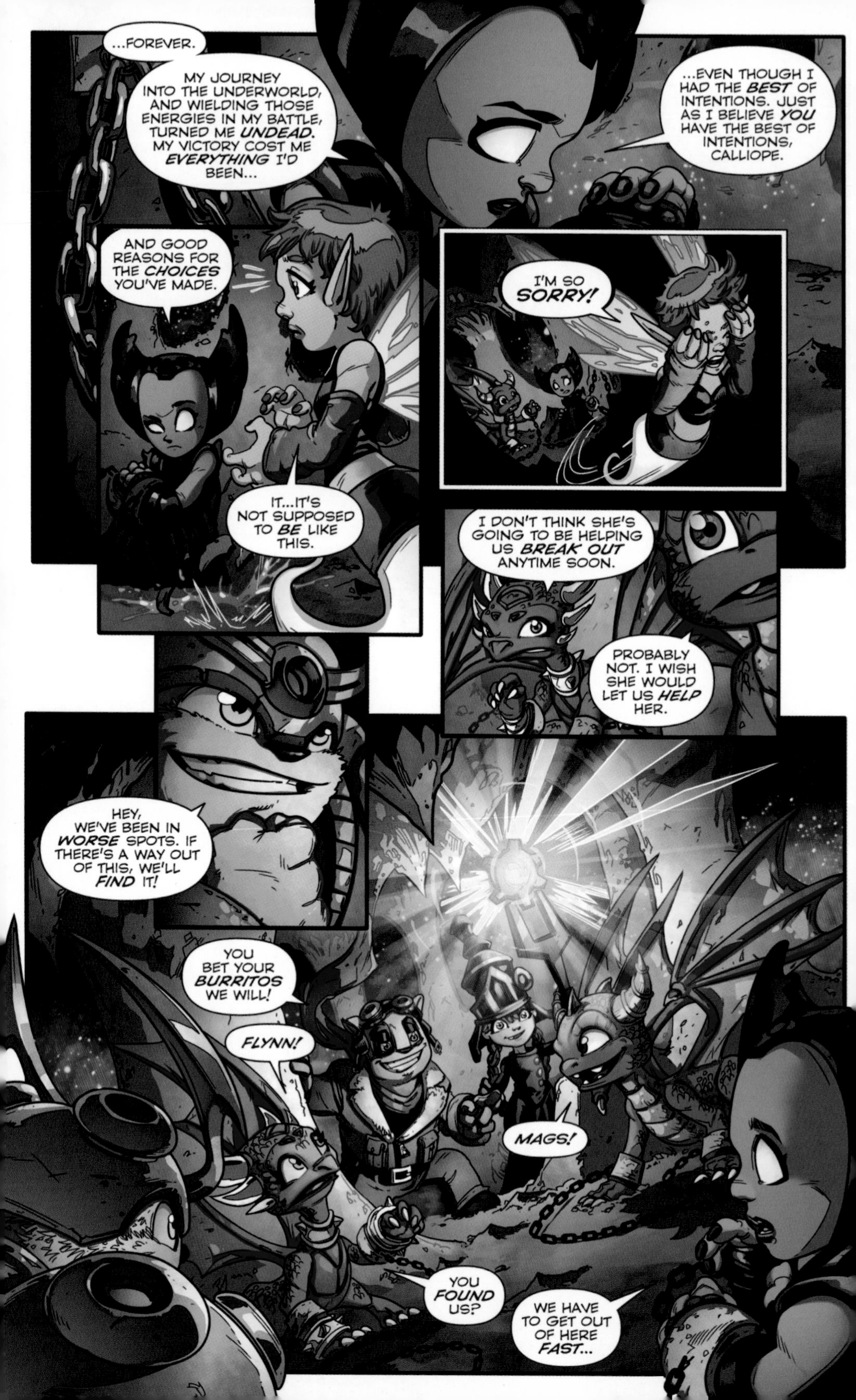
...FOREVER.
MY JOURNEY INTO THE UNDERWORLD, AND WIELDING THOSE ENERGIES IN MY BATTLE, TURNED ME UNDEAD. MY VICTORY COST ME EVERYTHING I'D BEEN...
...EVEN THOUGH I HAD THE BEST OF INTENTIONS. JUST AS I BELIEVE YOU HAVE THE BEST OF INTENTIONS, CALLIOPE.
AND GOOD REASONS FOR THE CHOICES YOU'VE MADE.
IT...IT'S NOT SUPPOSED TO BE LIKE THIS.
I'M SO SORRY!
I DON'T THINK SHE'S GOING TO BE HELPING US BREAK OUT ANYTIME SOON.
PROBABLY NOT. I WISH SHE WOULD LET US HELP HER.
HEY, WE'VE BEEN IN WORSE SPOTS. IF THERE'S A WAY OUT OF THIS, WE'LL FIND IT!
YOU BET YOUR BURRITOS WE WILL!
FLYNN!
MAGS!
YOU FOUND US?
WE HAVE TO GET OUT OF HERE FAST...

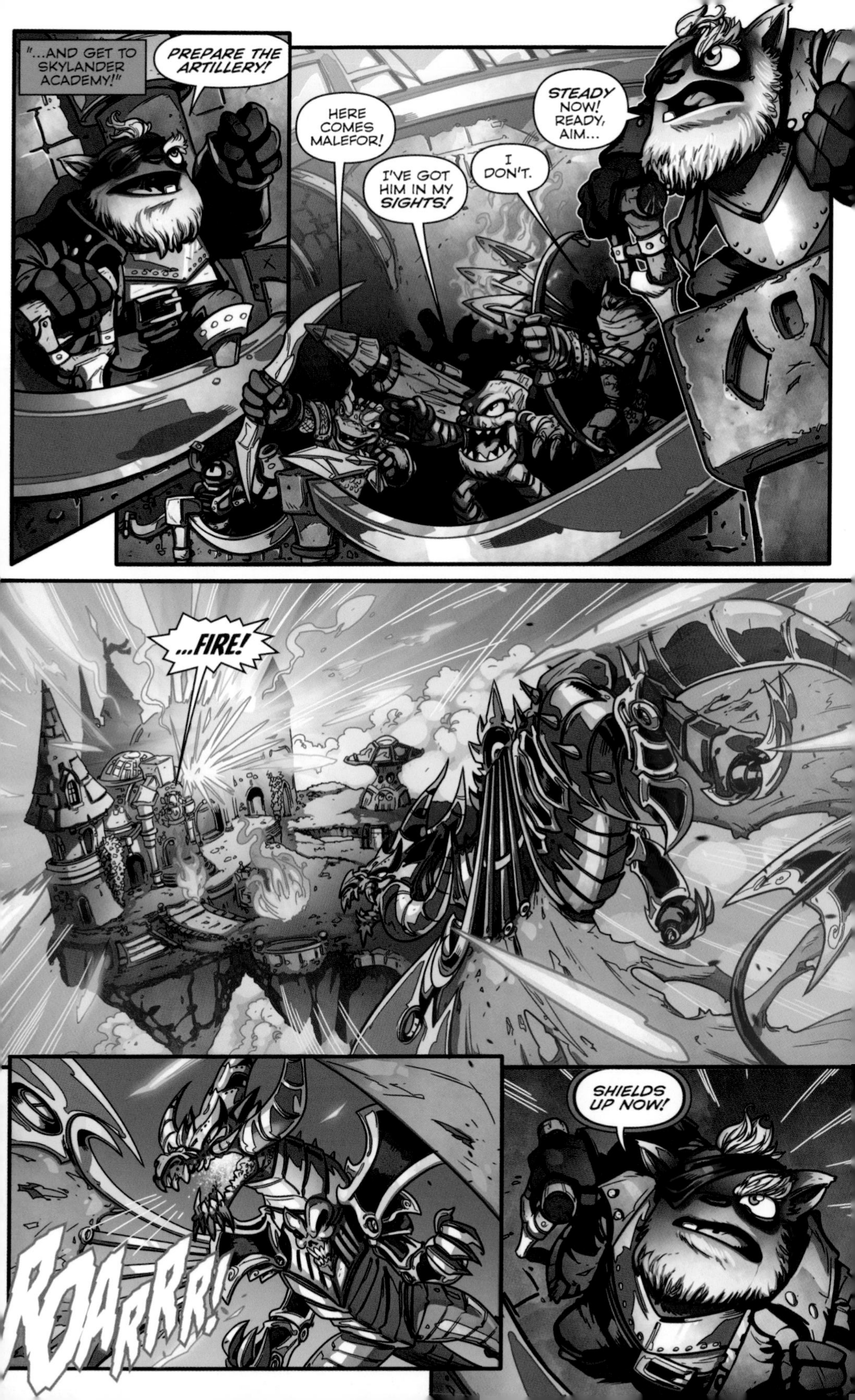
"...AND GET TO SKYLANDER ACADEMY!"
PREPARE THE ARTILLERY!
HERE COMES MALEFOR!
I'VE GOT HIM IN MY SIGHTS!
I DON'T.
STEADY NOW! READY, AIM...
...FIRE!
ROARRR!
SHIELDS UP NOW!

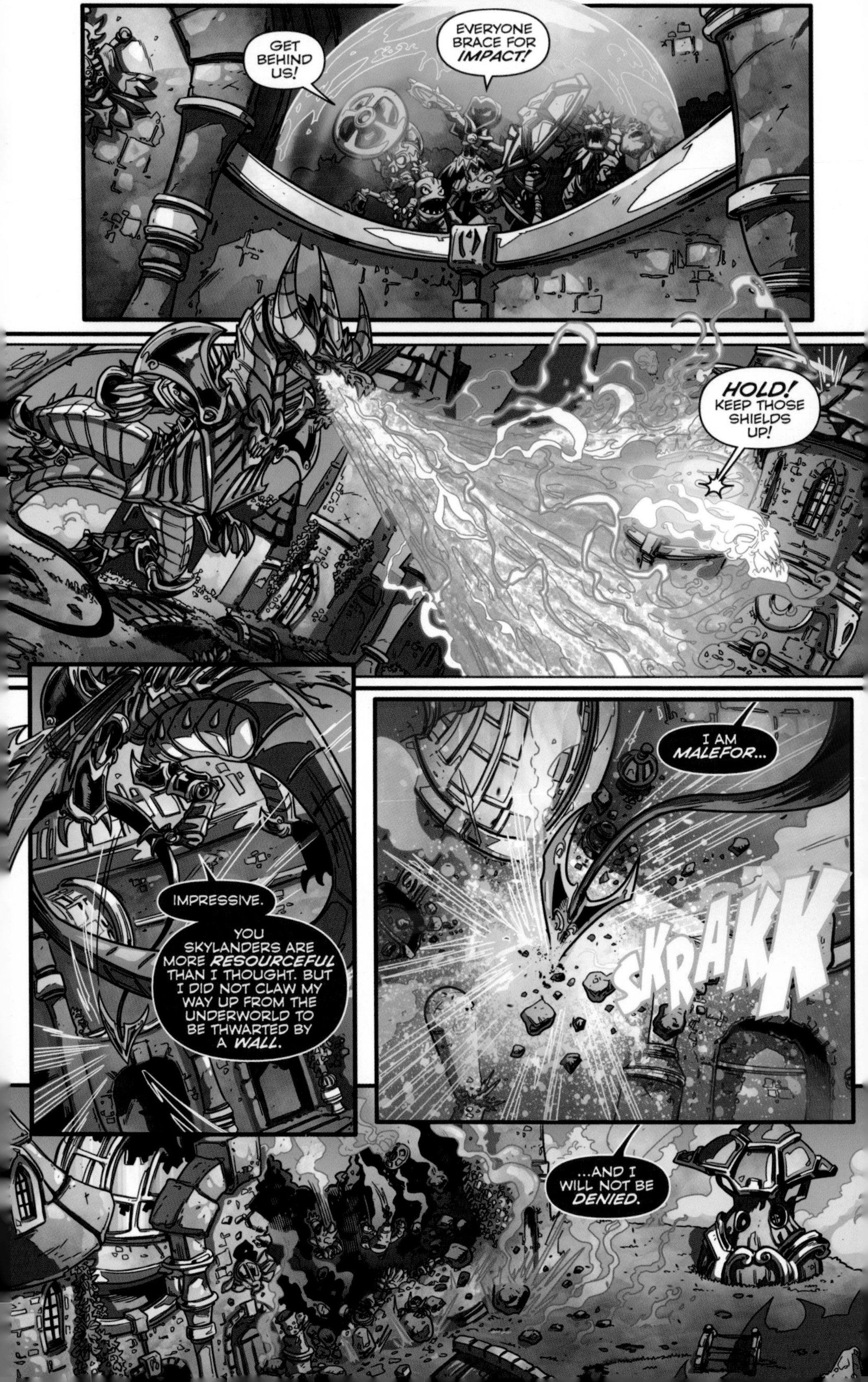
GET BEHIND US!
EVERYONE BRACE FOR IMPACT!
HOLD! KEEP THOSE SHIELDS UP!
IMPRESSIVE.
YOU SKYLANDERS ARE MORE RESOURCEFUL THAN I THOUGHT. BUT I DID NOT CLAW MY WAY UP FROM THE UNDERWORLD TO BE THWARTED BY A WALL.
I AM MALEFOR...
SKRAKK
...AND I WILL NOT BE DENIED.

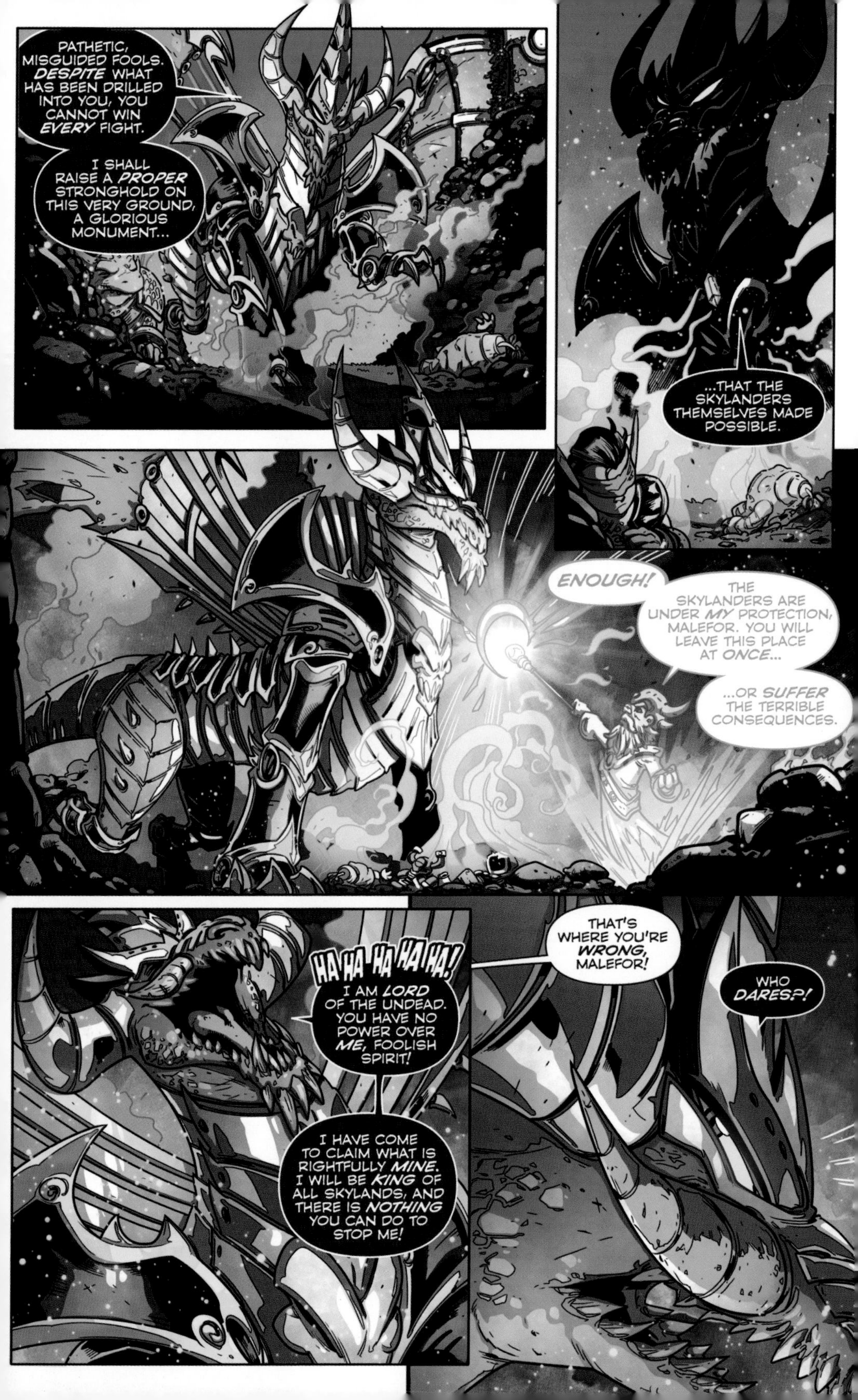
PATHETIC, MISGUIDED FOOLS. DESPITE WHAT HAS BEEN DRILLED INTO YOU, YOU CANNOT WIN EVERY FIGHT.
I SHALL RAISE A PROPER STRONGHOLD ON THIS VERY GROUND, A GLORIOUS MONUMENT...
...THAT THE SKYLANDERS THEMSELVES MADE POSSIBLE.
ENOUGH!
THE SKYLANDERS ARE UNDER MY PROTECTION, MALEFOR. YOU WILL LEAVE THIS PLACE AT ONCE...
...OR SUFFER THE TERRIBLE CONSEQUENCES.
HA HA HA HA HA!
I AM LORD OF THE UNDEAD. YOU HAVE NO POWER OVER ME, FOOLISH SPIRIT!
I HAVE COME TO CLAIM WHAT IS RIGHTFULLY MINE. I WILL BE KING OF ALL SKYLANDS, AND THERE IS NOTHING YOU CAN DO TO STOP ME!
THAT'S WHERE YOU'RE WRONG, MALEFOR!
WHO DARES?!

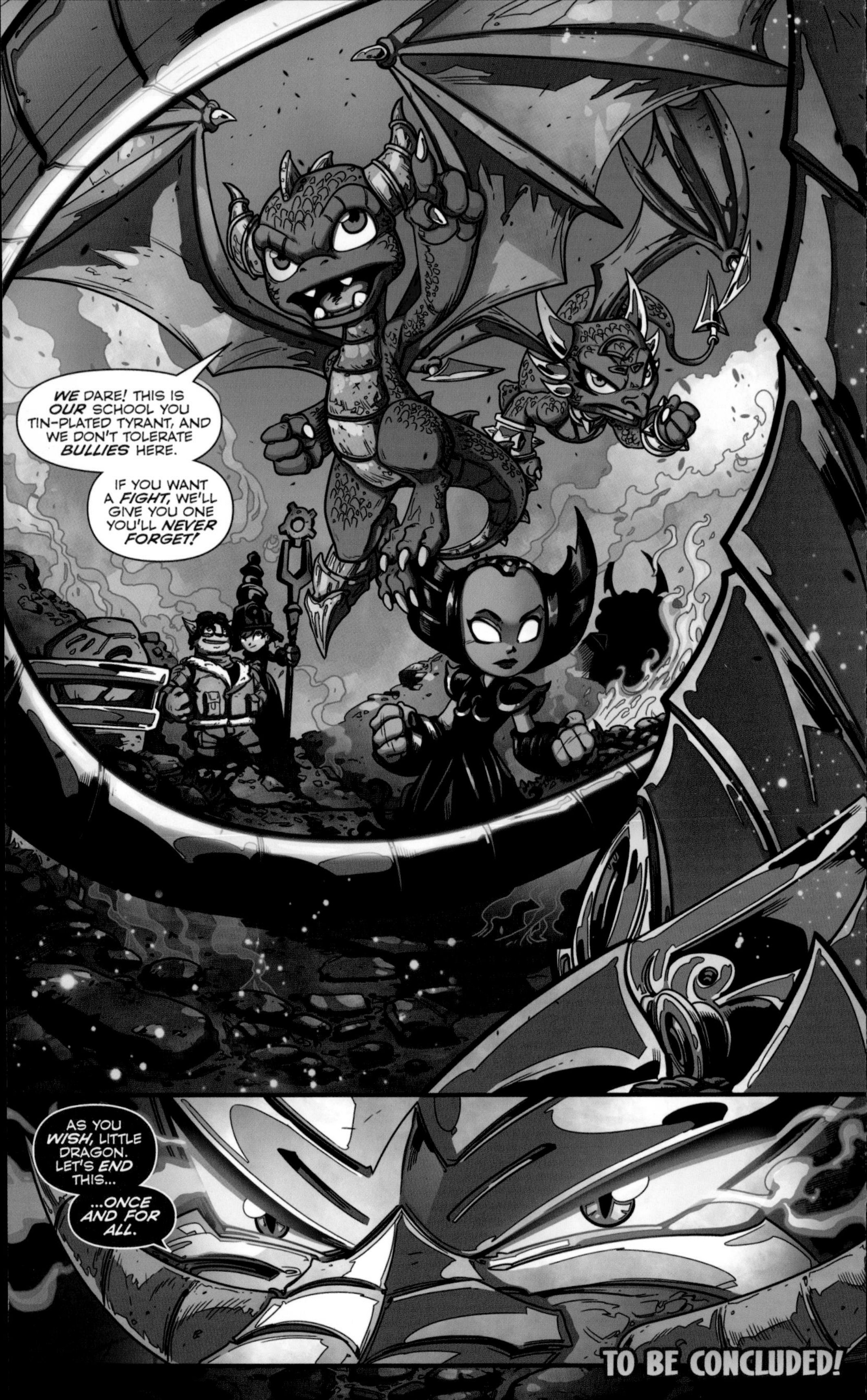
WE DARE! THIS IS OUR SCHOOL YOU TIN-PLATED TYRANT, AND WE DON'T TOLERATE BULLIES HERE.
IF YOU WANT A FIGHT, WE'LL GIVE YOU ONE YOU'LL NEVER FORGET!
AS YOU WISH, LITTLE DRAGON. LET'S END THIS...
...ONCE AND FOR ALL.
TO BE CONCLUDED!

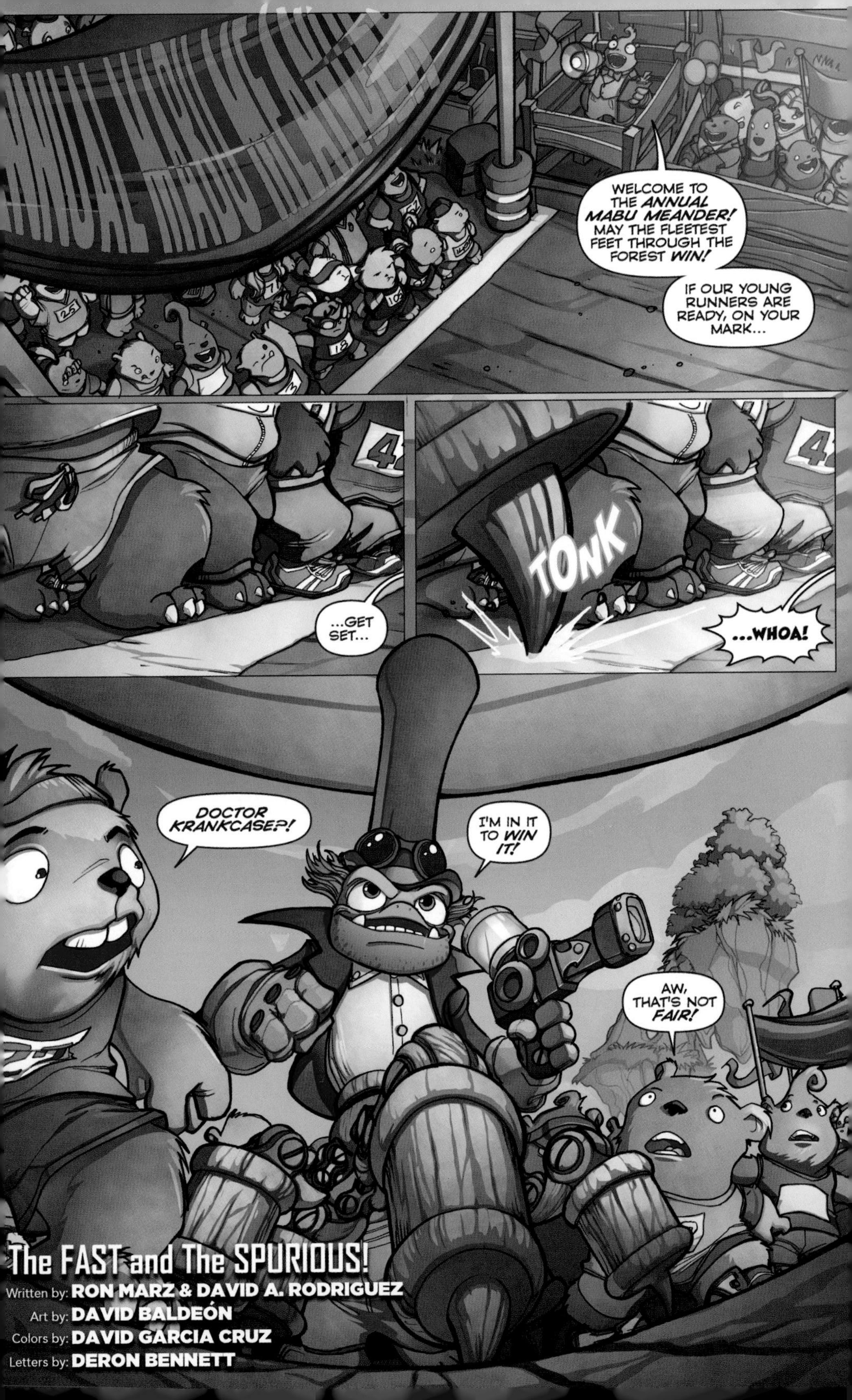
WELCOME TO THE ANNUAL MABU MEANDER! MAY THE FLEETEST FEET THROUGH THE FOREST WIN!
IF OUR YOUNG RUNNERS ARE READY, ON YOUR MARK...
...GET SET...
TONK
...WHOA!
DOCTOR KRANKCASE?!
I'M IN IT TO WIN IT!
AW, THAT'S NOT FAIR!

The FAST and The SPURIOUS!

Written by: **RON MARZ & DAVID A. RODRIGUEZ**
Art by: **DAVID BALDEÓN**
Colors by: **DAVID GARCIA CRUZ**
Letters by: **DERON BENNETT**

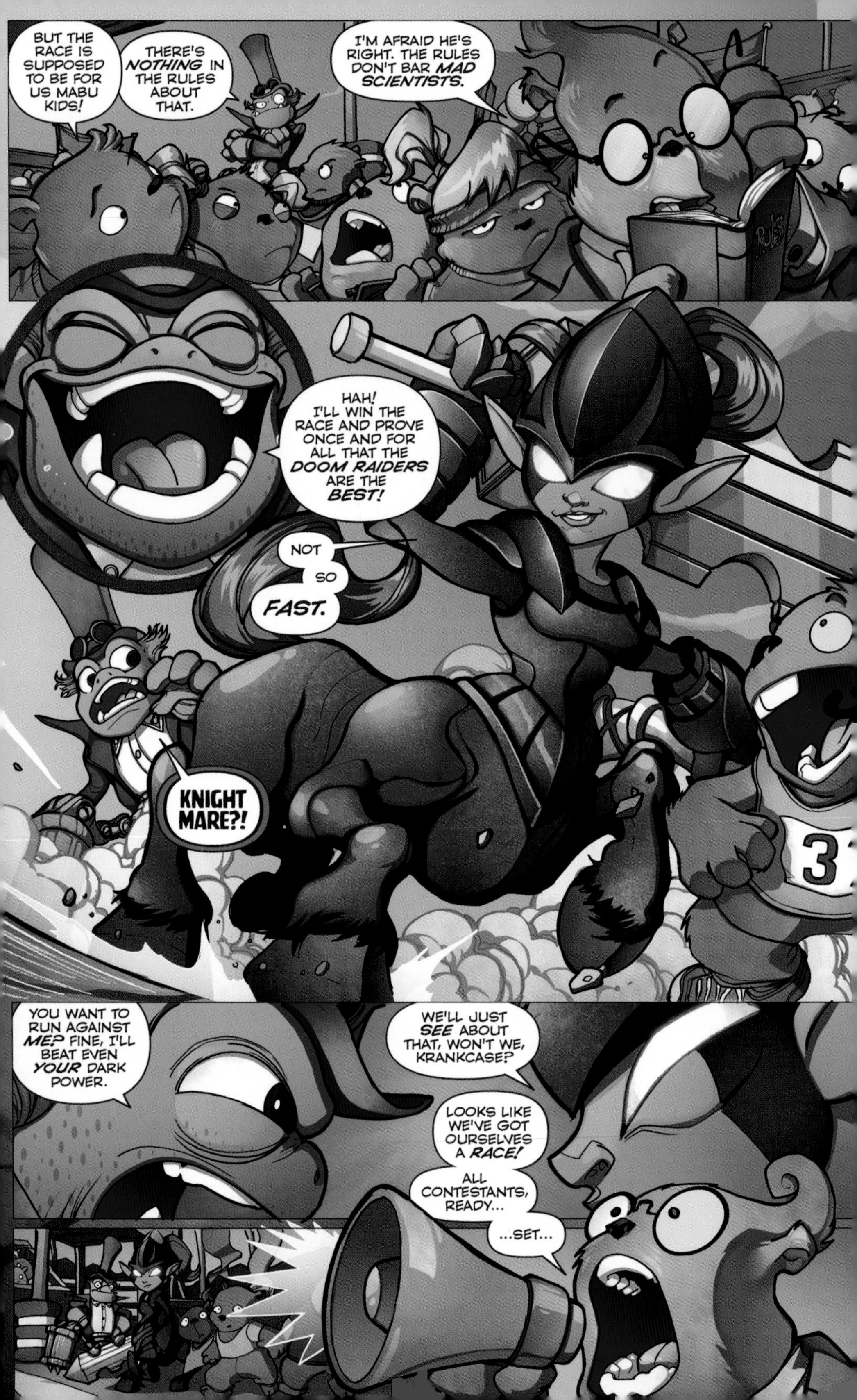
BUT THE RACE IS SUPPOSED TO BE FOR US MABU KIDS!
THERE'S *NOTHING* IN THE RULES ABOUT THAT.
I'M AFRAID HE'S RIGHT. THE RULES DON'T BAR *MAD SCIENTISTS*.
RULES
HAH! I'LL WIN THE RACE AND PROVE ONCE AND FOR ALL THAT THE *DOOM RAIDERS* ARE THE *BEST!*
NOT
SO
FAST.
KNIGHT MARE?!
3
YOU WANT TO RUN AGAINST *ME?* FINE, I'LL BEAT EVEN *YOUR* DARK POWER.
WE'LL JUST *SEE* ABOUT THAT, WON'T WE, KRANKCASE?
LOOKS LIKE WE'VE GOT OURSELVES A *RACE!*
ALL CONTESTANTS, READY...
...SET...

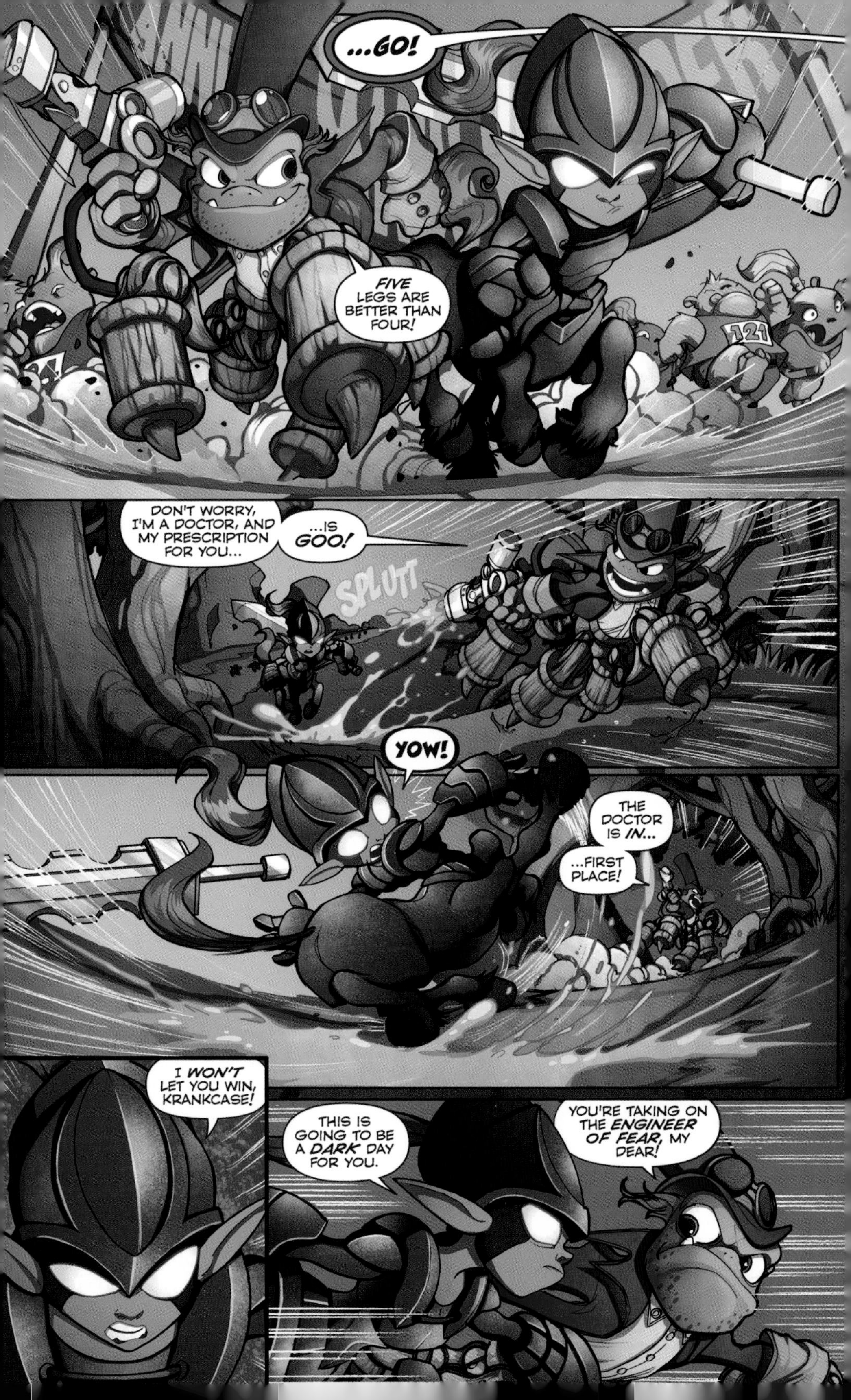
...GO!
FIVE LEGS ARE BETTER THAN FOUR!
121
DON'T WORRY, I'M A DOCTOR, AND MY PRESCRIPTION FOR YOU...
...IS GOO!
SPLUTT
YOW!
THE DOCTOR IS IN...
...FIRST PLACE!
I WON'T LET YOU WIN, KRANKCASE!
THIS IS GOING TO BE A DARK DAY FOR YOU.
YOU'RE TAKING ON THE ENGINEER OF FEAR, MY DEAR!

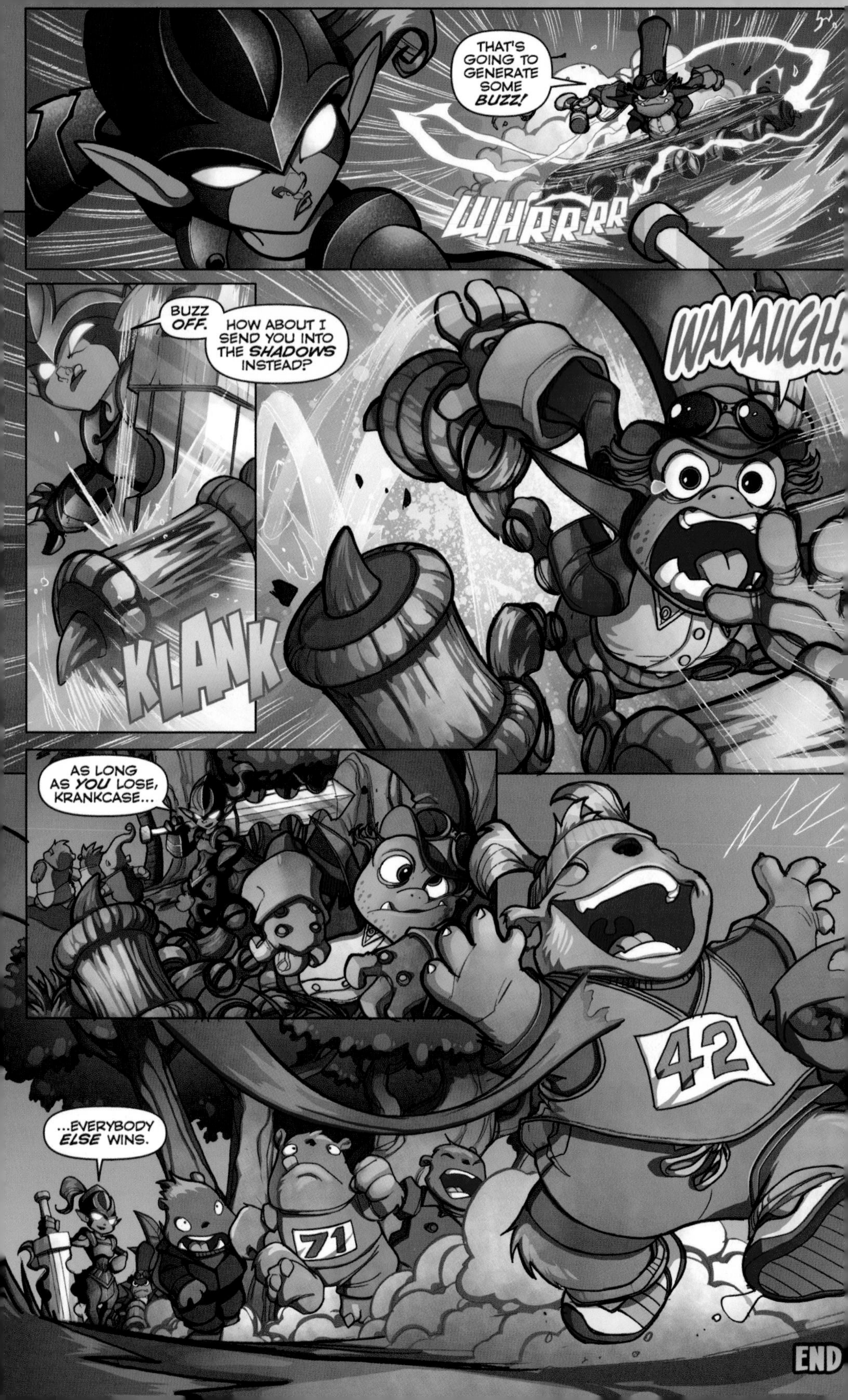
THAT'S GOING TO GENERATE SOME BUZZ!
WHRRRR
BUZZ OFF.
HOW ABOUT I SEND YOU INTO THE SHADOWS INSTEAD?
WAAAUGH!
KLANK
AS LONG AS YOU LOSE, KRANKCASE...
...EVERYBODY ELSE WINS.
42
71
END

SKYLANDERS™

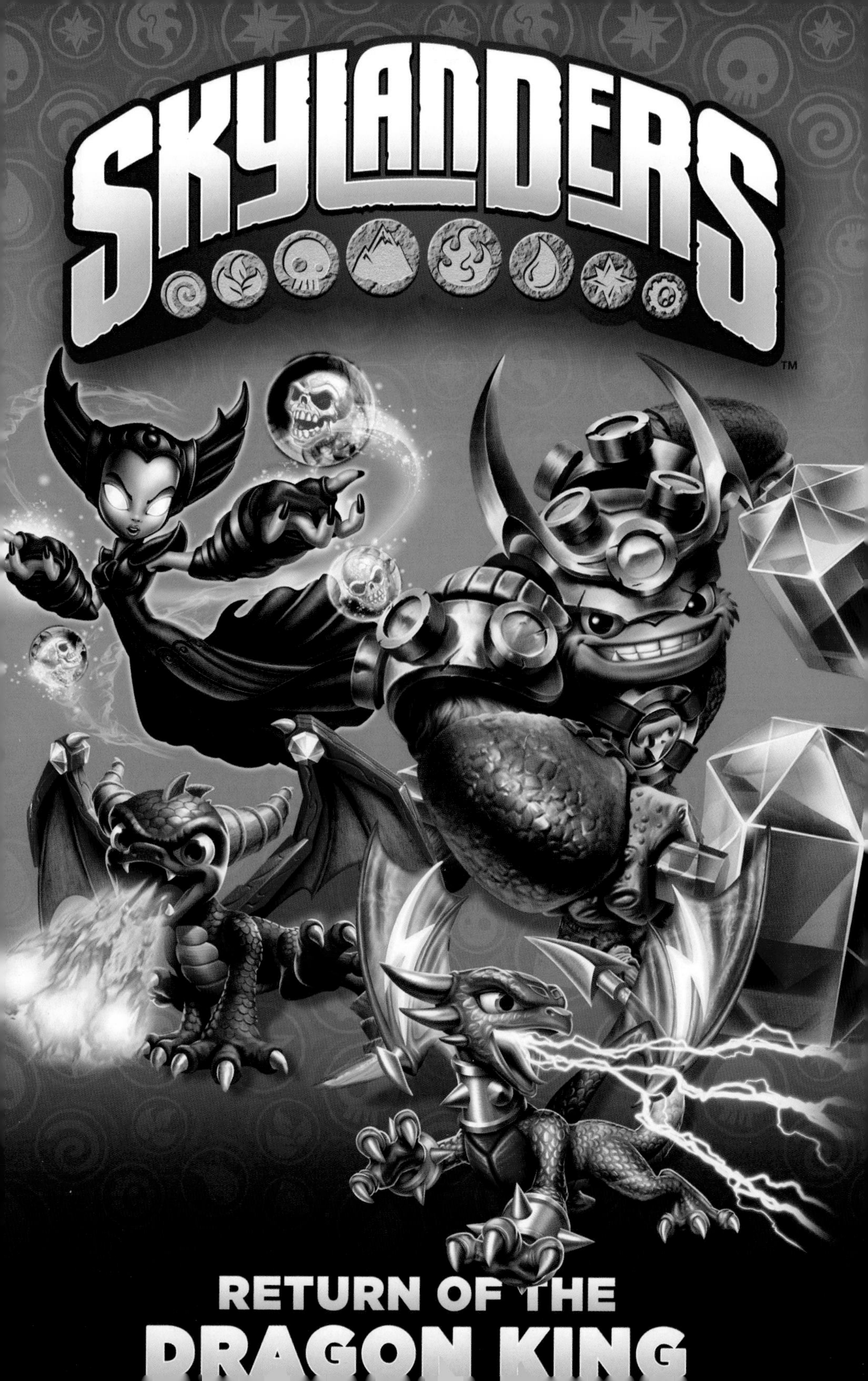

RETURN OF THE DRAGON KING

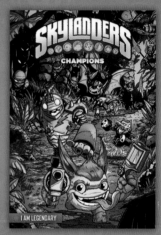